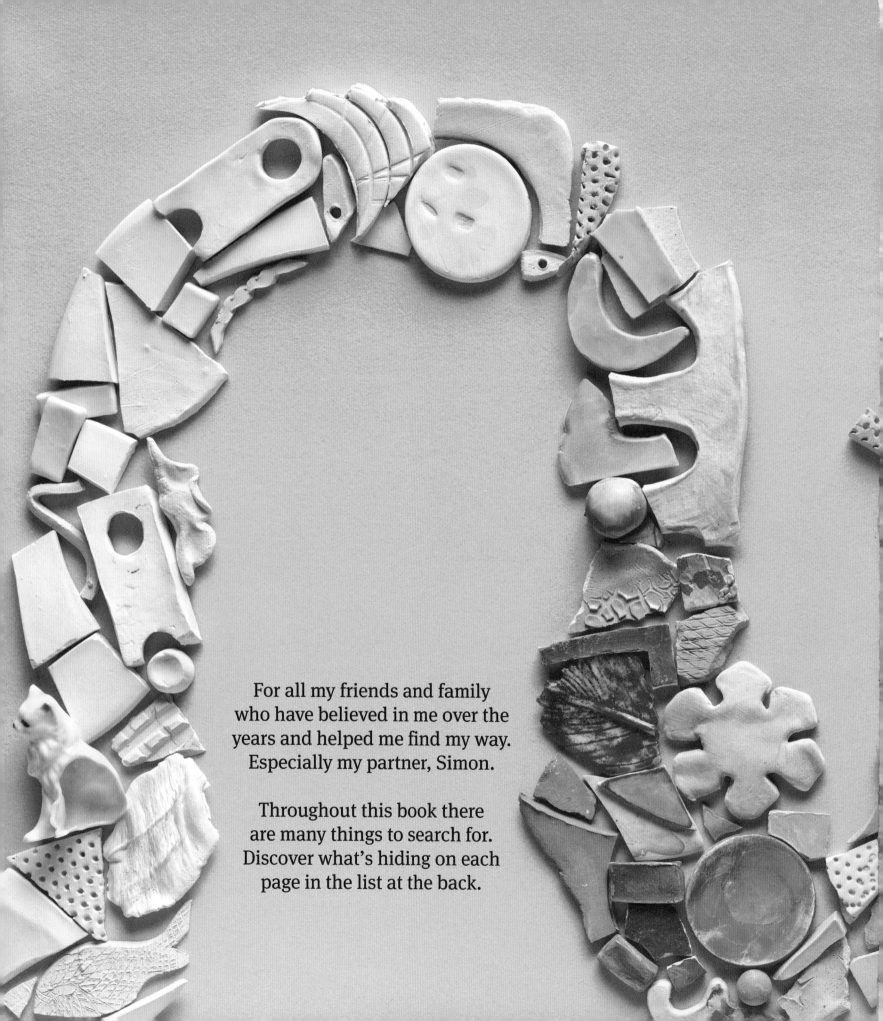

For all my friends and family who have believed in me over the years and helped me find my way. Especially my partner, Simon.

Throughout this book there are many things to search for. Discover what's hiding on each page in the list at the back.

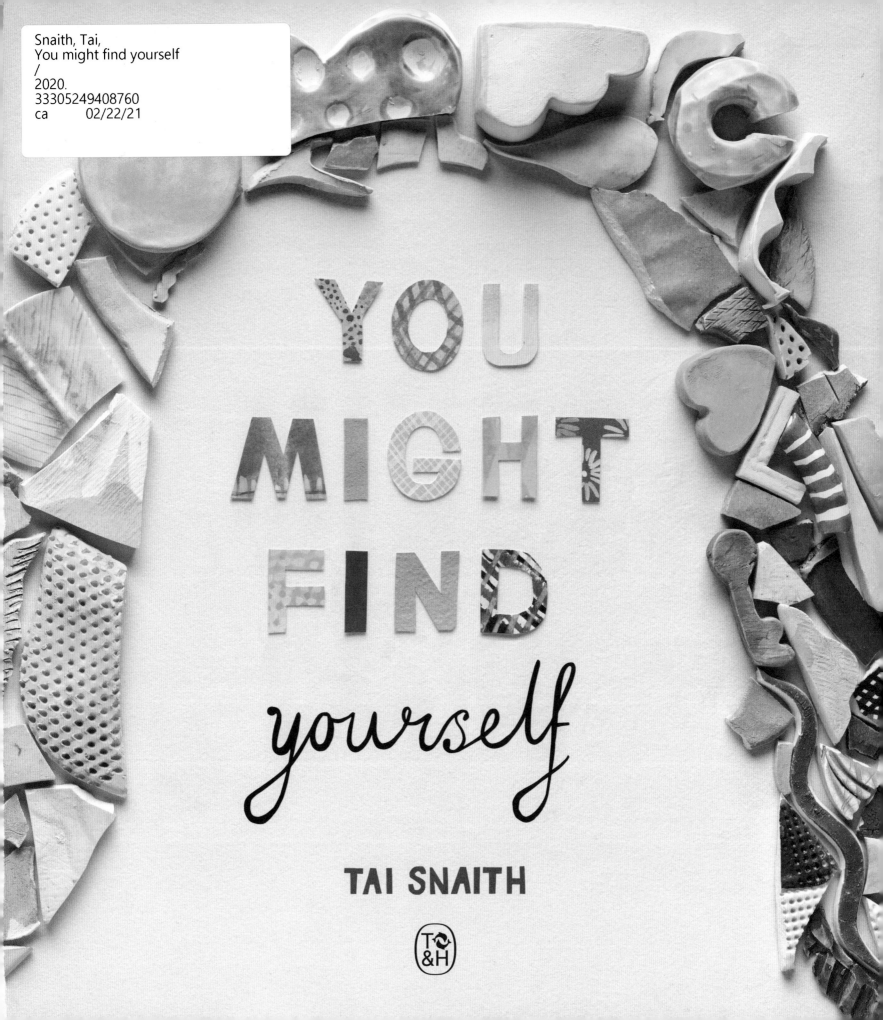

YOU MIGHT FIND *yourself*

TAI SNAITH

T&H

Life is like a winding path, with lots of different places to discover along the way.

If you could go anywhere,
imagine where you might find yourself.

You might find yourself
in a cool, shady place.

Imagine discovering all the curious creatures that live there.

Or, you might find yourself
in a bright, summery place.

Imagine what you might make
before it gets washed away.

You might find yourself
in a new friend's garden.

Imagine what you could do
to help keep it beautiful.

Or, you might find yourself
in a difficult situation where it hurts a lot.

Imagine a cuddle that will make you feel better.

You might find yourself
on a train full of thoughts,

imagining how it feels to be someone else.

You might find yourself
in a place that makes you feel very SMALL,

or a place that makes you feel like a GIANT!

You might find yourself

in a mysterious place

that you have never been before,

imagining what happened in the past.

Or, you might find yourself working hard and watching seeds sprout and come alive.

Imagine sharing what you grow with your neighbors.

You might find yourself

a little bit confused at times about which way to go.

Imagine what might
be down the road for you;

it may not always
be what you expect.

You might find yourself
in a faraway place, doing things you never thought possible.

Imagine eating green beans with a king and a queen!

Or, you might find yourself on a stage

You might find yourself
in an ancient, sacred place,

imagining the stories and
songs of that land and its people.

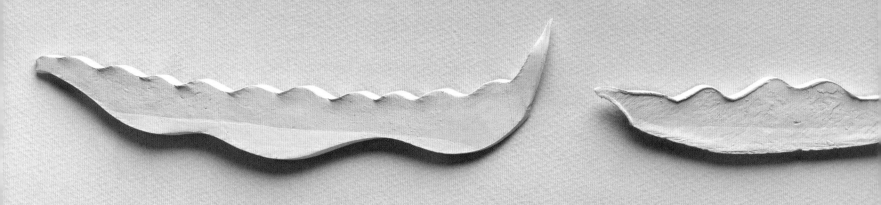

While on life's path,

you will find yourself

making lots of choices.

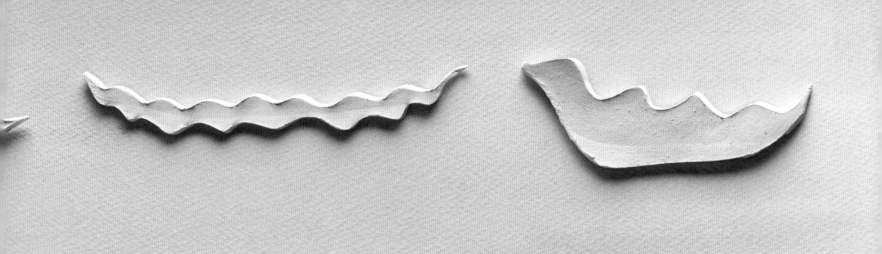

Imagine paving your own way.

But no matter where you might find yourself,
you're sure to meet many friends

who will help you on your way.

Together you might ask,

"Where should we go next?"

Extra things to THINK and DO
Ways to use your imagination to make the world better.

Things to do outside

Sometimes we make our houses so nice that we forget to leave them! Can you imagine a game you can play outside with your dolls or toys? Is there a part of your garden that could make a miniature world or landscape for your favourite toys?

find:

5 x

Amazing trees

Imagine if there were no more trees left in the world. Write about what that would be like. Imagine if the whole world was a forest. Write about what that would be like. Can you think of a spot where you can plant a new tree?

FIND:

2 x

Nothing is permanent except change

One thing about our world that always stays the same is that everything is changing, all the time. Can you think of how you might change as a person in the future? What kind of changes would you like to make to the world around you?

find:

5 x

Plastic-free oceans

The ocean is someone's home, too. Think of all the creatures that live there: fish, octopuses, whales, coral. Imagine if your home was full of rubbish and bits of plastic. Next time you go to the beach, try to pick up five pieces of plastic from the sand or water.

find:

8 x

Bye-bye pain

One way to make the feeling of pain, hurt or loneliness go away is to think about the feeling of love. Can you close your eyes and think of someone who loves you? Can you draw a picture of them? When you notice someone close to you is sad, remind them that you love them.

FIND:

6 x

Secret thoughts

First imagine what other people in the room or in your class are thinking. It's impossible to know! Now think about something really silly or funny or naughty in your own mind and notice how no one can tell what you're thinking. You can guess what someone else is thinking, but unless you talk about it together, you never really know.

find:

7 x PT

Scale and power

Sometimes it feels like everything around us is made for humans. Imagine if you were a tiny animal, what animal would you be? How big and scary would a human foot look to you? Write a story about it.

FIND:

3 x

can you FIND all the hidden THINGS?

Finding clues

Keep an eye out for broken, old things. Imagine you are a detective. Sometimes you might find a glass bottle from the olden days or a piece of a broken plate. Clean them up and spend some time thinking about who might have owned them and what they were used for. You could make a time capsule and bury it for future kids to discover what it was like to be alive now.

find:
6 x

Music of the future

What do you think instruments will look like in the future? How will they work? Can you make the sound of music from the future? Can you design your own futuristic instrument?

find:
8 x

Seedbank

Collect the seeds from plants and flowers at the end of summer, dry them in paper bags and once they are dried, store them in labelled jars. You can plant them again next autumn or spring. You can also start a seedbank in your classroom and begin a garden at your school! Share what you grow with your friends and family.

FIND:
6 x
4 x

First Peoples

Do you know the history of the place where you live? Can you imagine what it was like for the first people who lived there? Learn the Indigenous name for the place you live. If you are Indigenous yourself, you could share your knowledge of country with your teacher and your class.

FIND:
1 x

Choose your own adventure

Sometimes there are two paths you can take. Tell or write a short story about what might be down a particular path and where it might take you. Think about where else in the world you would like to go and what you might find there.

find:
5 x

Paving your own way

Every day we make important choices about how we live: the materials we use to make things, the food we eat, the way we treat others. These choices affect our lives. Can you think of a choice that can change how you or someone else feels? What is the best choice you made today?

find:
6 x
3 x
2 x
4 x
2 x

Trying new things

Imagine how boring it would be if we ate only one colour of food. Whether it be trying a new vegetable or even just a different way to walk home from school, trying new things can make life a whole lot more interesting. Can you think of a meal that has every colour of the rainbow?

find:
2 x

Collaboration

Working together with friends to create something or make something happen is called collaboration. Try a game where one person draws a series of squiggles and the other person joins them together to make a picture. Sometimes putting two brains together is much better than one.

FIND:
6 x

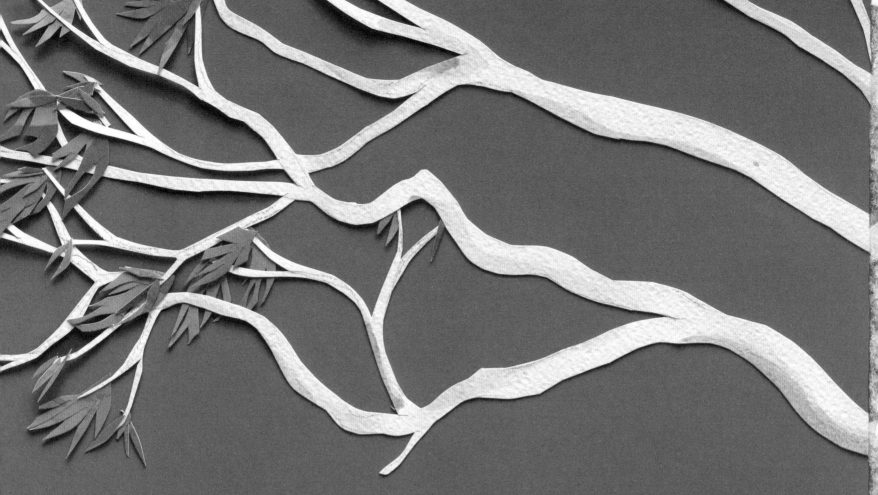

Photo: Tom Ross

A note from the author

I find myself living with my two beautiful boys, Leo (who is nine and designed the vampire alien) and Gil (who is six and came up with the hologram guitar), our cat Malcolm, our puppy Wally, and our blue-tongue lizard Clampy in our very own giant doll's house designed by their dad and my partner, Simon Knott (he lives here, too). We live on Wurundjeri land on the banks of the Merri Merri (creek), which is the path of an ancient volcano flow and the site of thousands of years of Indigenous culture and history.

In our backyard stands a majestic, white lemon-scented gum tree that sheds its bark once a year in summer, like a lizard shedding its skin, and is home to a powerful owl who keeps watch over us all. There are quite a few pictures in the book inspired by my own friends, house and life. I feel very lucky to live the life I do – I can't imagine a more magical place to find myself!

First published in 2019 in Australia by Thames
& Hudson Australia Pty Ltd, 11 Central
Boulevard, Portside Business Park, Port
Melbourne, Victoria 3207

First published in 2020 in the United States of
America by Thames & Hudson Inc., 500 Fifth
Avenue, New York, New York 10110

www.thamesandhudsonusa.com

ISBN 978-1-76076-033-5

Library of Congress Control Number:
2019951704

Every effort has been made to trace accurate
ownership of copyrighted text and visual
materials used in this book. Errors or omissions
will be corrected in subsequent editions,
provided notification is sent to the publisher.

Design: Hope Lumsden-Barry
Editing: Jaclyn Crupi
Photography: Matthew Stanton
Printed and bound in China by C&C

MIX
Paper from
responsible sources
FSC® C008047

FSC® is dedicated to the promotion of
responsible forest management worldwide. This
book is made of material from FSC®-certified
forests and other controlled sources.